APOLLO

For my incredible agent and friend, Lilly Ghahremani. I am so grateful for our musical friendship.

—R. S. R.

In memory of my friend Kim. May you dance and swing with the stars.

—K. D.

BEACH LANE BOOKS
An imprint of Simon & Schuster Children's Publishing Division
1230 Avenue of the Americas, New York, New York 10020

Book design by Rebecca Syracuse

For information about special discounts for bulk purchases, please contact Simon & Schuster Special Sales at 1-866-506-1949 or business@simonandschuster.com.
Simon & Schuster strongly believes in freedom of expression and stands against censorship in all its forms. For more information, visit BooksBelong.com.
The Simon & Schuster Speakers Bureau can bring authors to your live event. For more information or to book an event, contact the Simon & Schuster Speakers Bureau at 1-866-248-3049 or visit our website at www.simonspeakers.com.
The text for this book was set in American Typewriter.
The illustrations for this book were rendered digitally.
Manufactured in China
0625 SCP
First Edition
10 9 8 7 6 5 4 3 2 1
Library of Congress Cataloging-in-Publication Data
Names: Rajan, Rekha S., author. | Daley, Ken, 1976- illustrator.
Title: That swingin' sound! : the musical friendship of Ella Fitzgerald and Louis Armstrong / written by Rekha S. Rajan ; illustrated by Ken Daley.
Description: New York : Beach Lane Books, 2025. | Includes bibliographical references. | Audience: Ages 4–8 | Audience: Grades 2–3 | Summary: "A dual biography about jazz legends Ella Fitzgerald and Louis Armstrong, their rise to musical stardom, and their friendship"—Provided by publisher.
Identifiers: LCCN 2024045308 (print) | LCCN 2024045309 (ebook) | ISBN 9781665957038 (hardcover) | ISBN 9781665957045 (ebook)
Subjects: LCSH: Fitzgerald, Ella—Juvenile literature. | Armstrong, Louis,1901–1971—Juvenile literature. | Jazz musicians—United States—Biography—Juvenile literature. | Friendship—Juvenile literature.
Classification: LCC ML3929 .R35 2025 (print) | LCC ML3929 (ebook) | DDC 782.42165092/2 [B]—dc23/eng/20240927
LC record available at https://lccn.loc.gov/2024045308
LC ebook record available at https://lccn.loc.gov/2024045309

Written by Rekha S. Rajan Illustrated by Ken Daley

That Swingin' Sound

The Musical Friendship of Ella Fitzgerald and Louis Armstrong

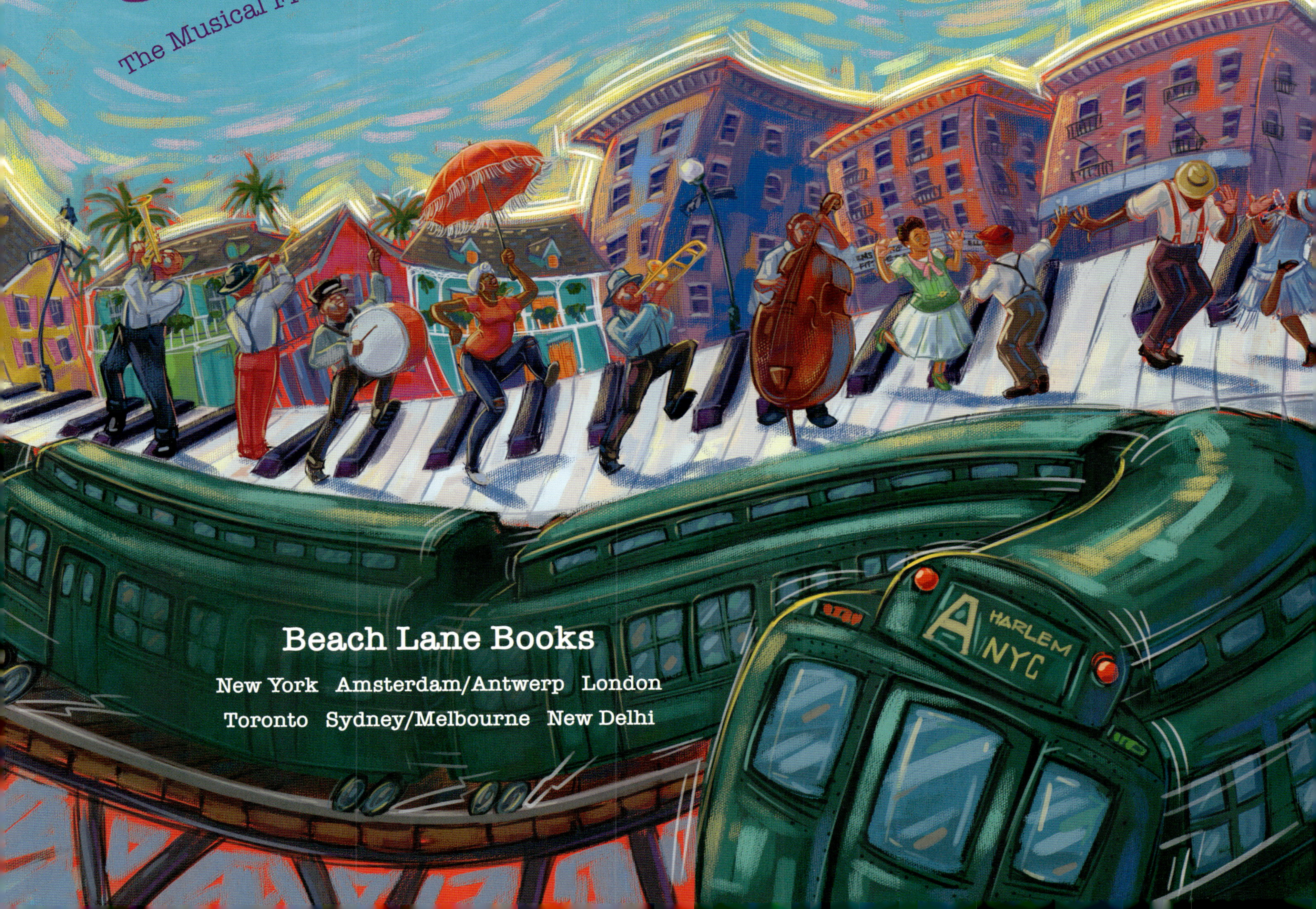

Beach Lane Books
New York Amsterdam/Antwerp London
Toronto Sydney/Melbourne New Delhi

HARLEM
A
NYC

Ella Fitzgerald loved to dance.

When little Ella heard jazz music, she stood on her tiptoes and twirled around the room. She felt the music notes move her legs as she danced as gracefully as a bluebird flying through the skies.

Ella danced everywhere.
At home, on the streets, with
her friends,

and on the train as it swayed into Harlem, New York, where she watched singers and dancers at the famous Apollo Theater.

Ella dreamed of her chance to be onstage. Every day, Ella danced next to her small bed in the orphanage. The other orphans joined in when Ella danced! They took turns snapping their fingers and swaying their hips to the sounds of the train tracks that rattled outside.

Ella wasn't sure if she was good enough to perform at the Apollo. But Ella didn't give up. Ella kept dancing.

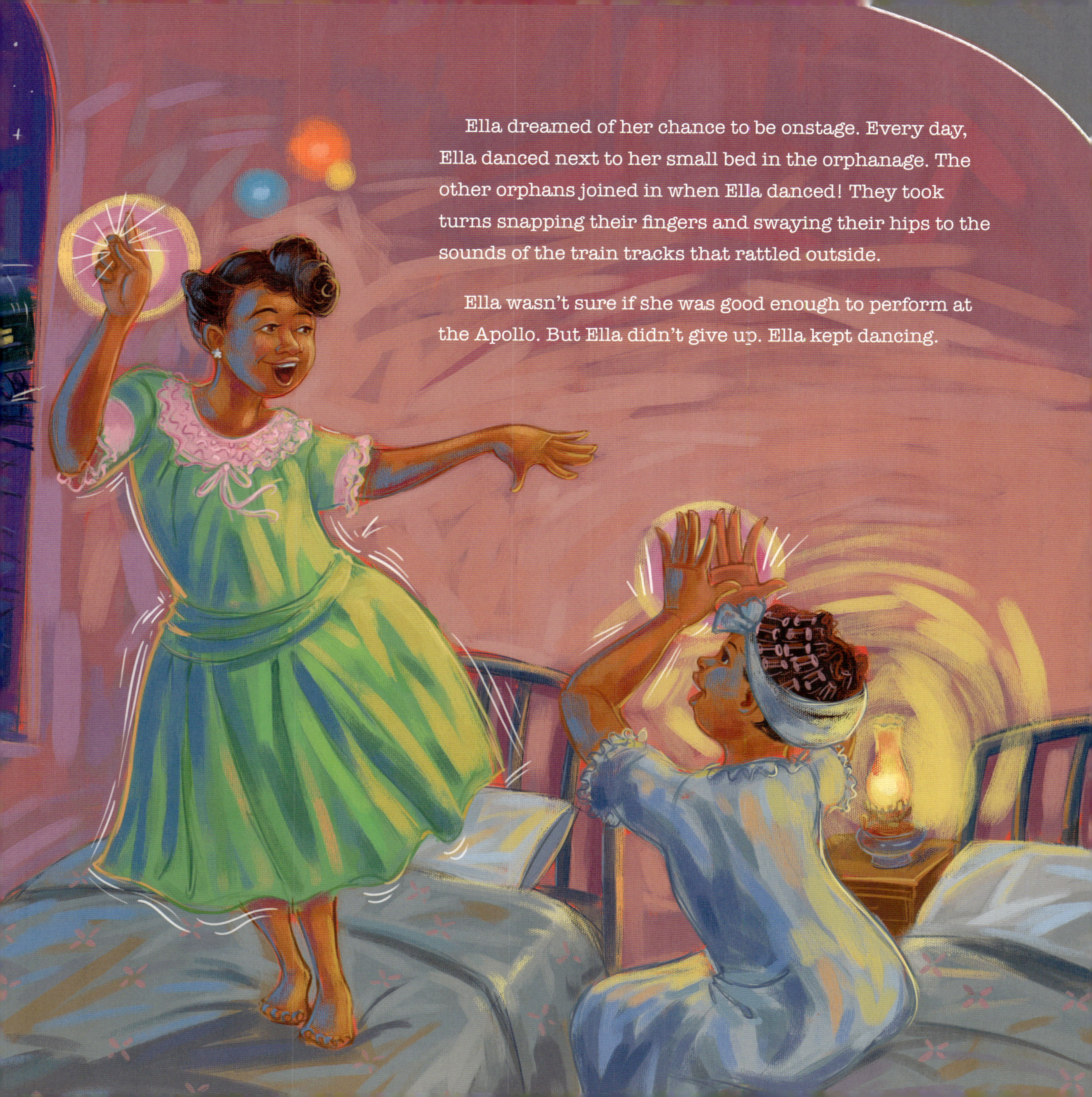

Way down south,
Louis Armstrong
was singing.

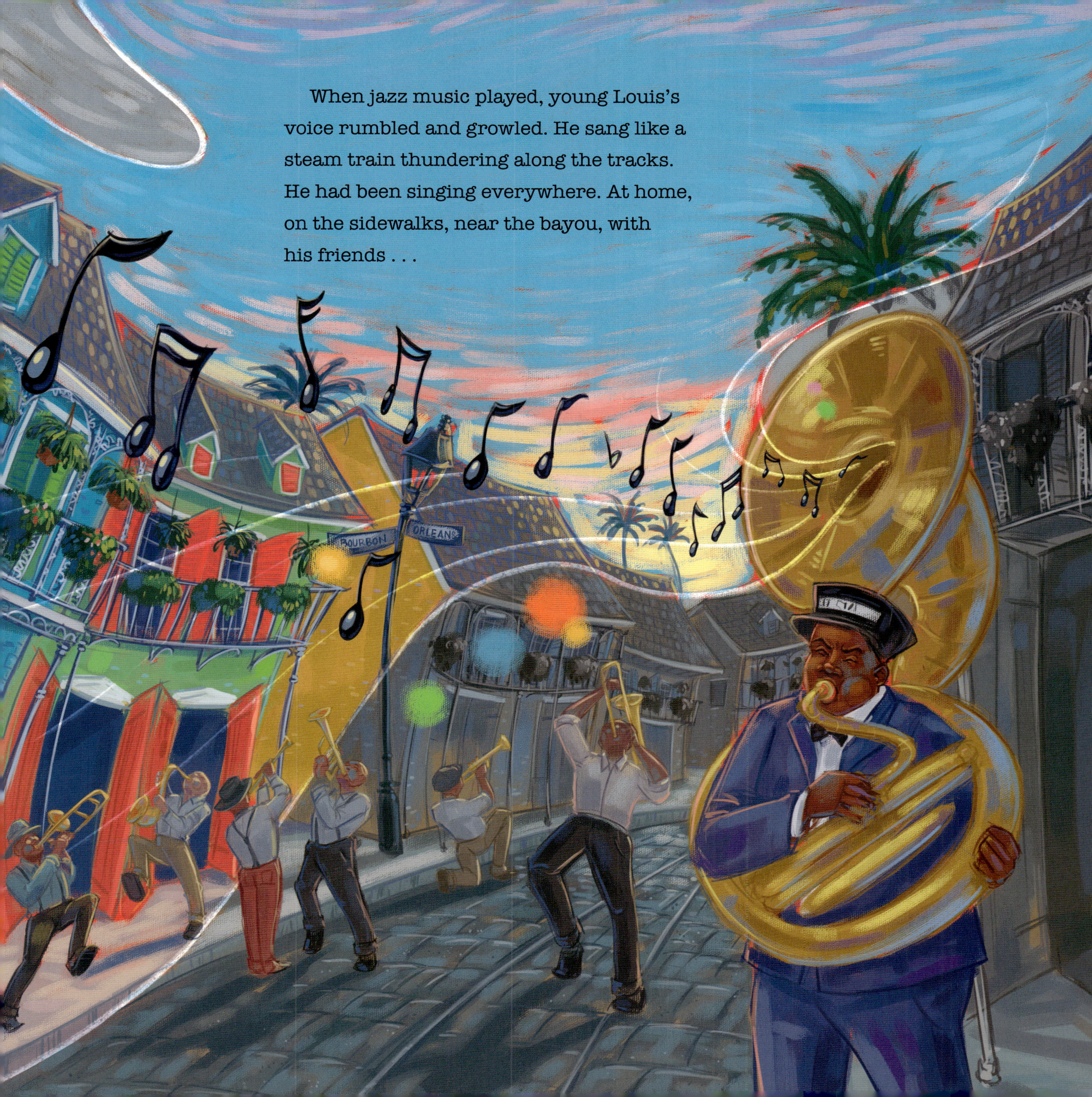

When jazz music played, young Louis's voice rumbled and growled. He sang like a steam train thundering along the tracks. He had been singing everywhere. At home, on the sidewalks, near the bayou, with his friends . . .

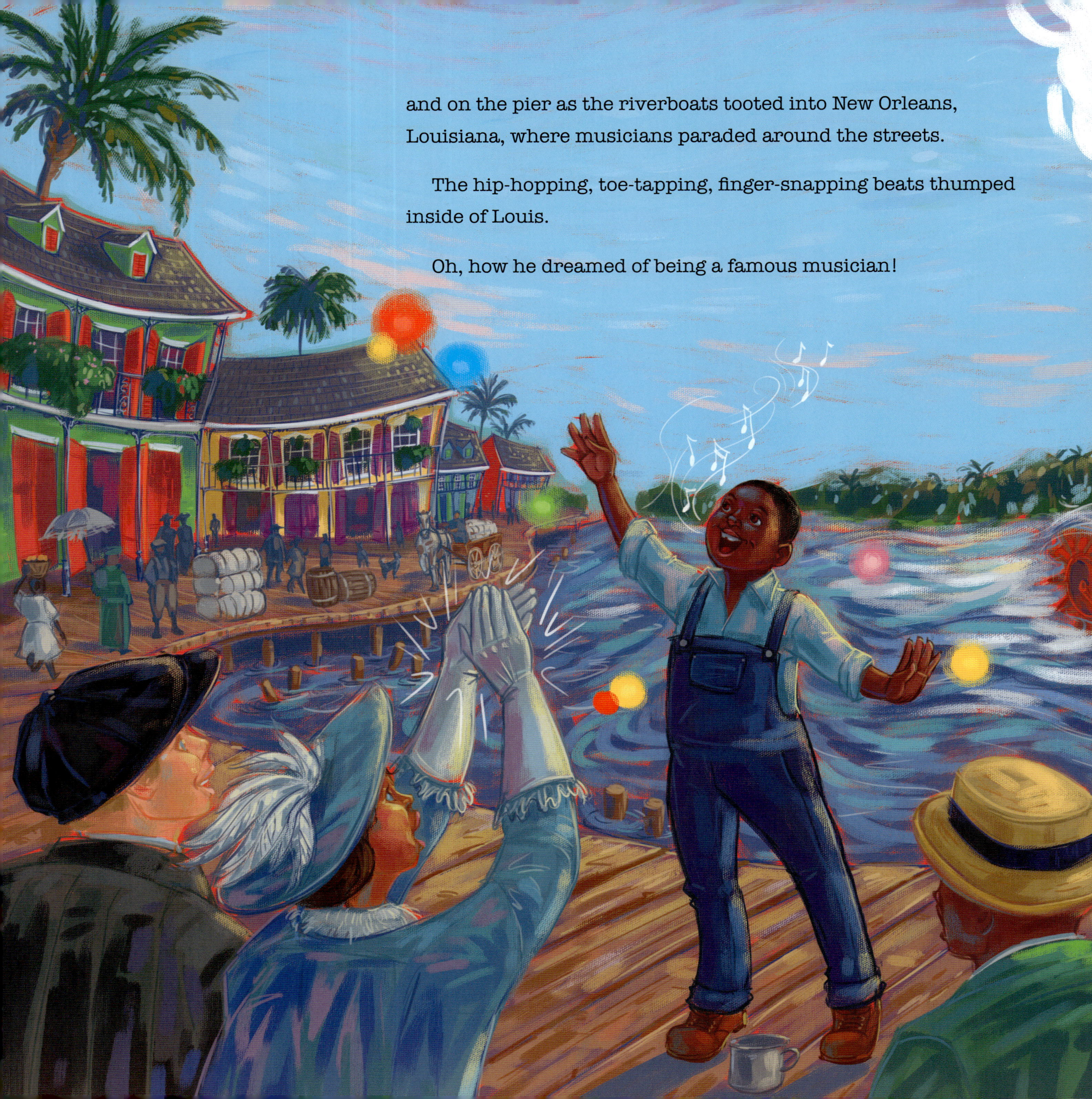

and on the pier as the riverboats tooted into New Orleans, Louisiana, where musicians paraded around the streets.

The hip-hopping, toe-tapping, finger-snapping beats thumped inside of Louis.

Oh, how he dreamed of being a famous musician!

Singing on street corners was hard work, but Louis didn't give up.

Louis kept singing.

Back up north in New York City, young Ella was always in the audience at the Apollo Theater. She saw singers and dancers and magicians. Oh, how she wanted to be on that stage!

When the theater director was choosing performers for a big competition, Ella crossed her fingers, toes, and her heart, wishing to be picked . . .

And she was!

She was ready to show everyone her moves. But the Edwards Sisters went onstage first. They were the best dancers in town, and Ella was worried she might not be good enough to win.

But then she thought of how music played inside of her.

She felt the music notes start to move from her toes, up her legs, into her lungs, and then—Ella decided to try something new.

Ella sang.

She made the notes sway as the strings plucked and the piano bounced. Ella could make the music notes fly from her mouth faster than her feet could move when dancing. She would scat up and down the musical scale:

"Ba-da-ba-dee-ba-da-doop-bop."

The audience cheered!

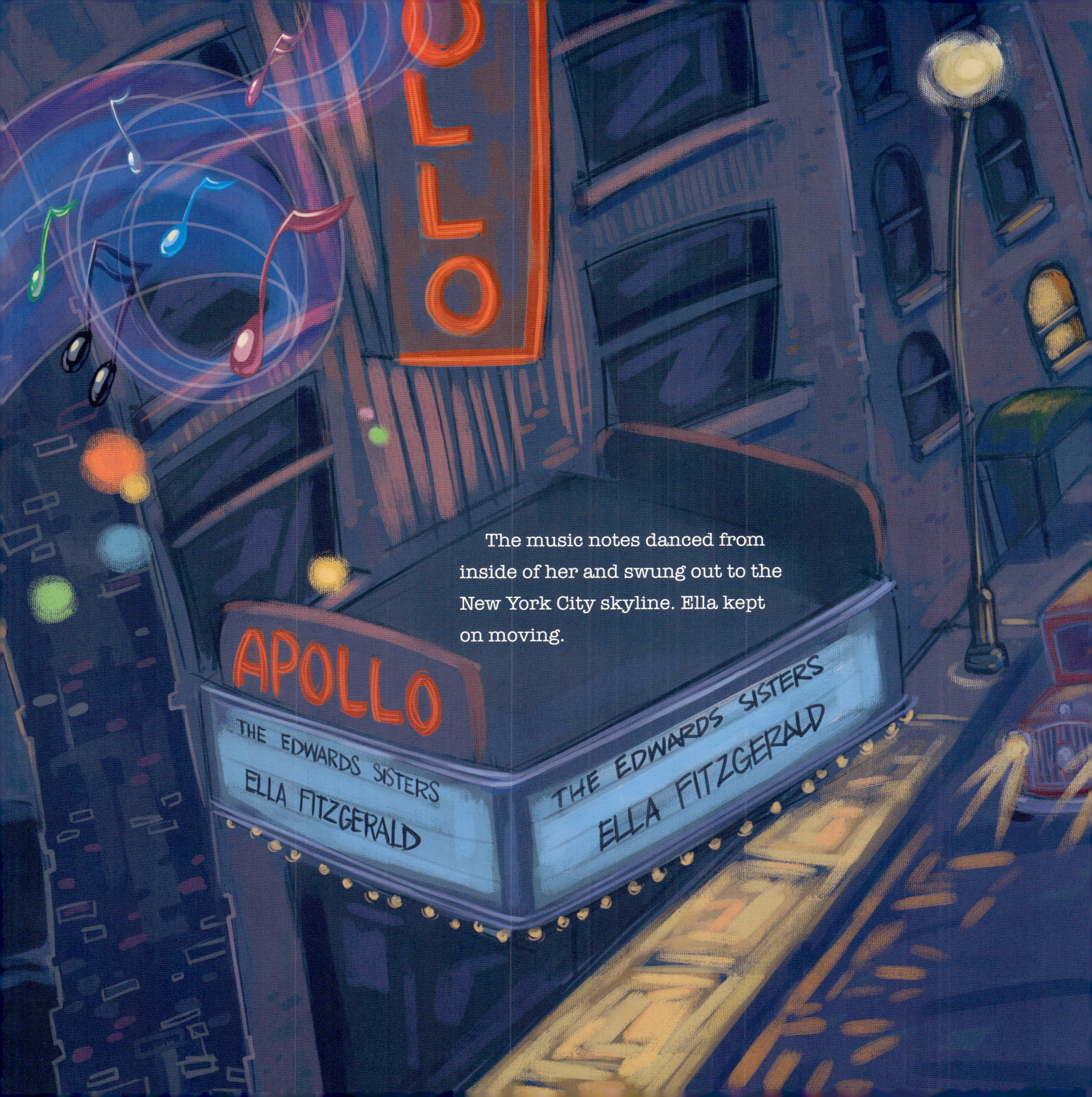

The music notes danced from inside of her and swung out to the New York City skyline. Ella kept on moving.

Louis was still singing all around New Orleans! Sometimes he even skipped school just to sing and make some extra money. Louis's gravelly voice shook out music notes that rang louder than the afternoon church bells.

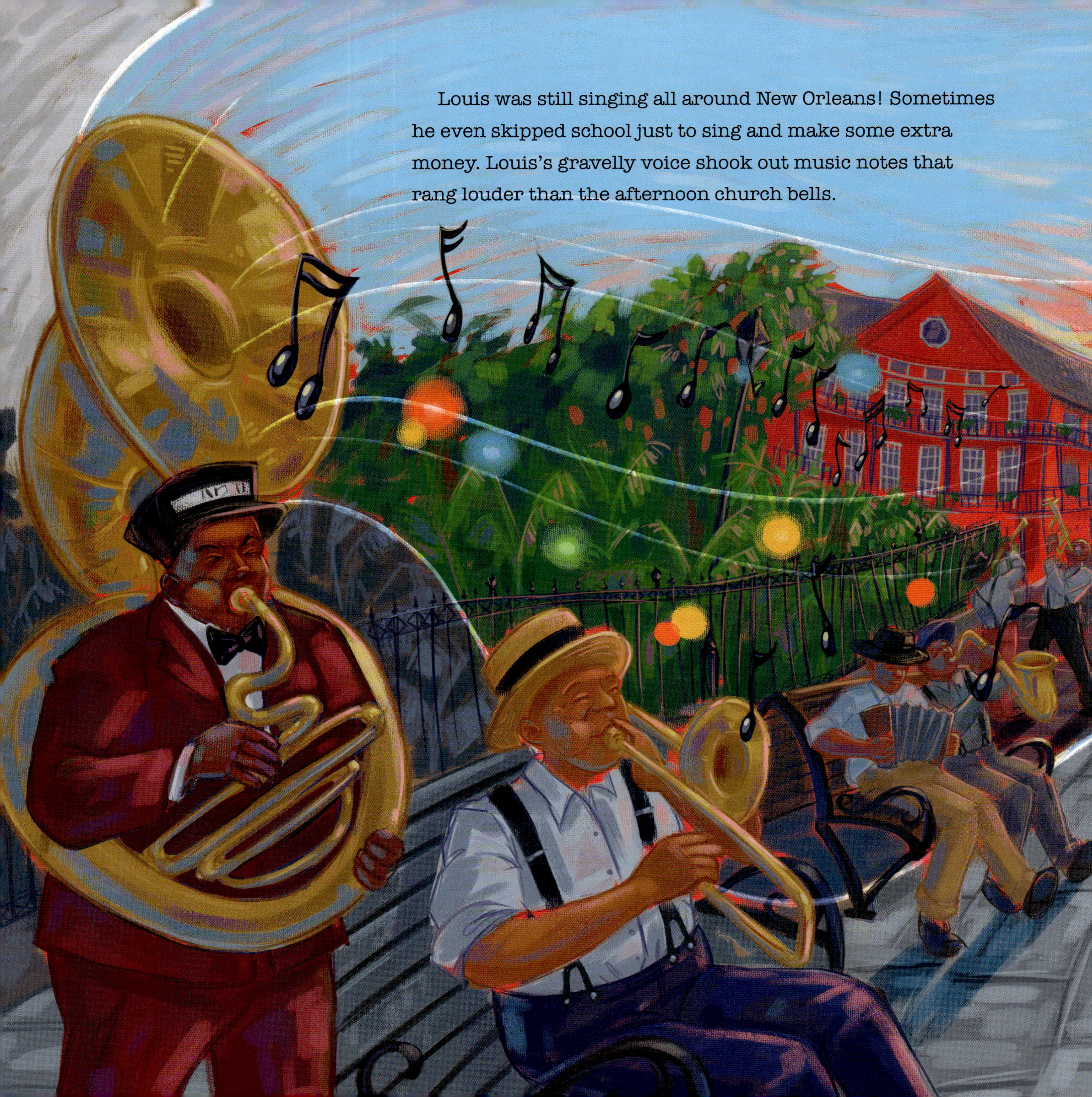

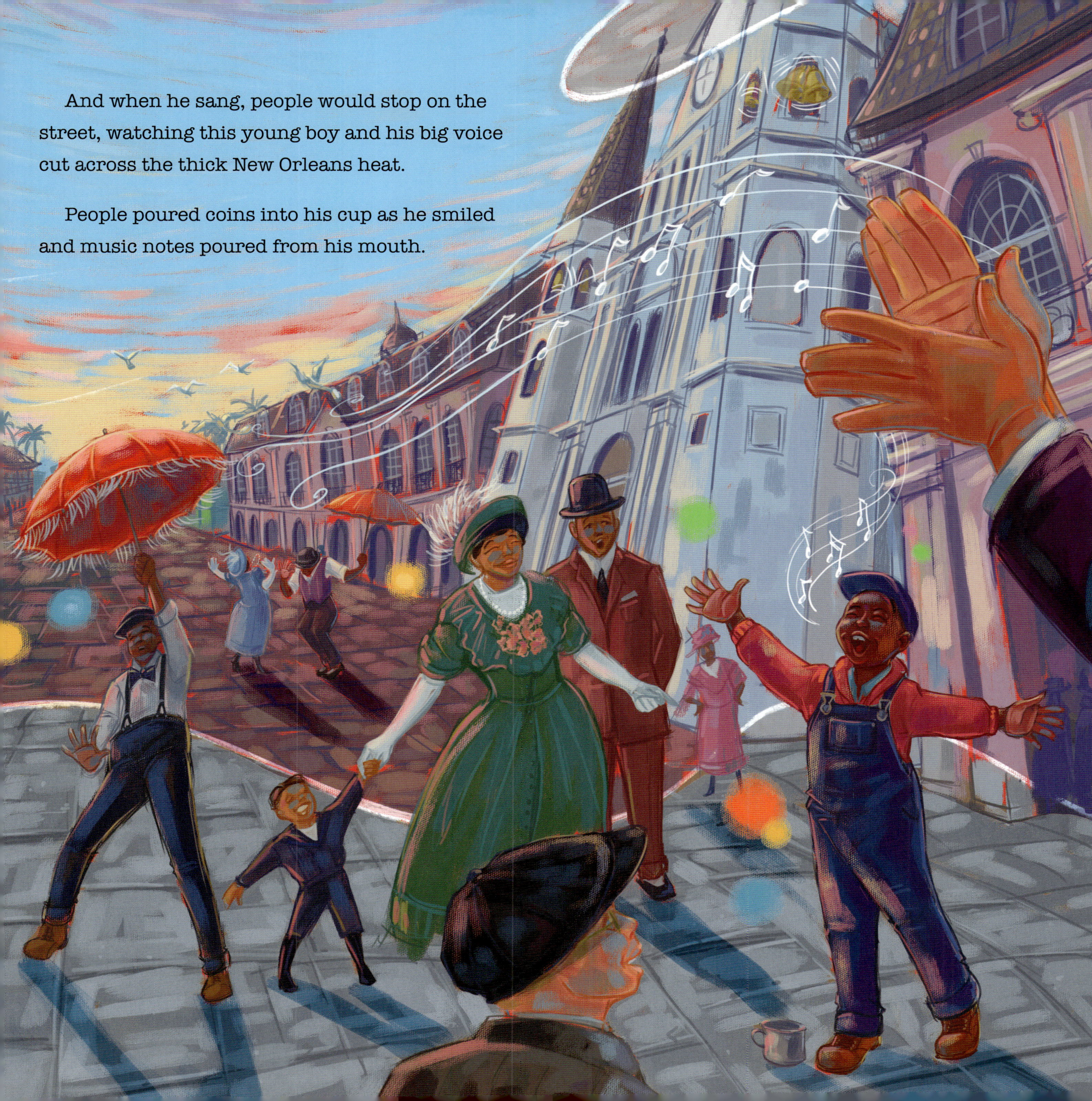

And when he sang, people would stop on the street, watching this young boy and his big voice cut across the thick New Orleans heat.

People poured coins into his cup as he smiled and music notes poured from his mouth.

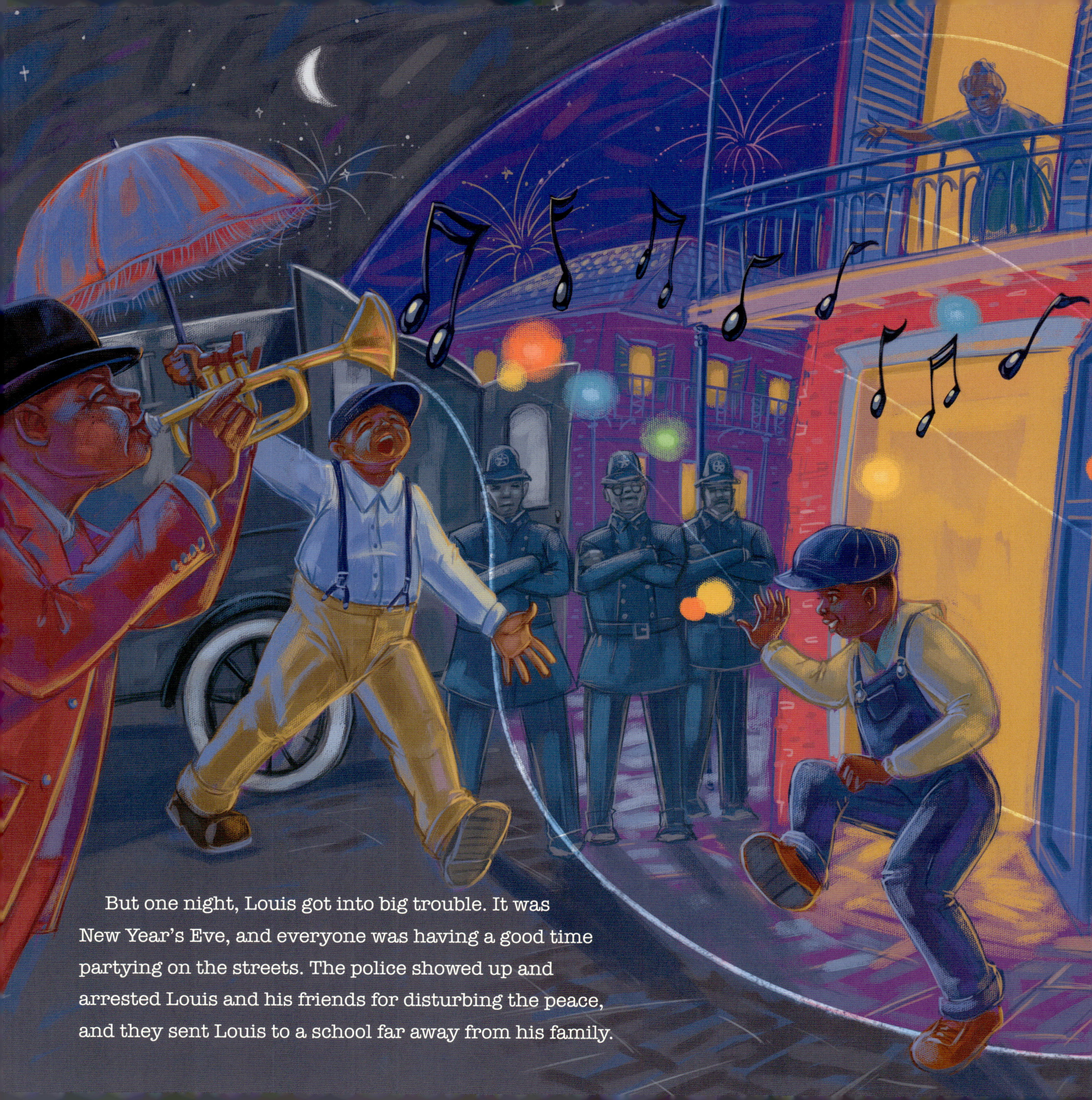

But one night, Louis got into big trouble. It was New Year's Eve, and everyone was having a good time partying on the streets. The police showed up and arrested Louis and his friends for disturbing the peace, and they sent Louis to a school far away from his family.

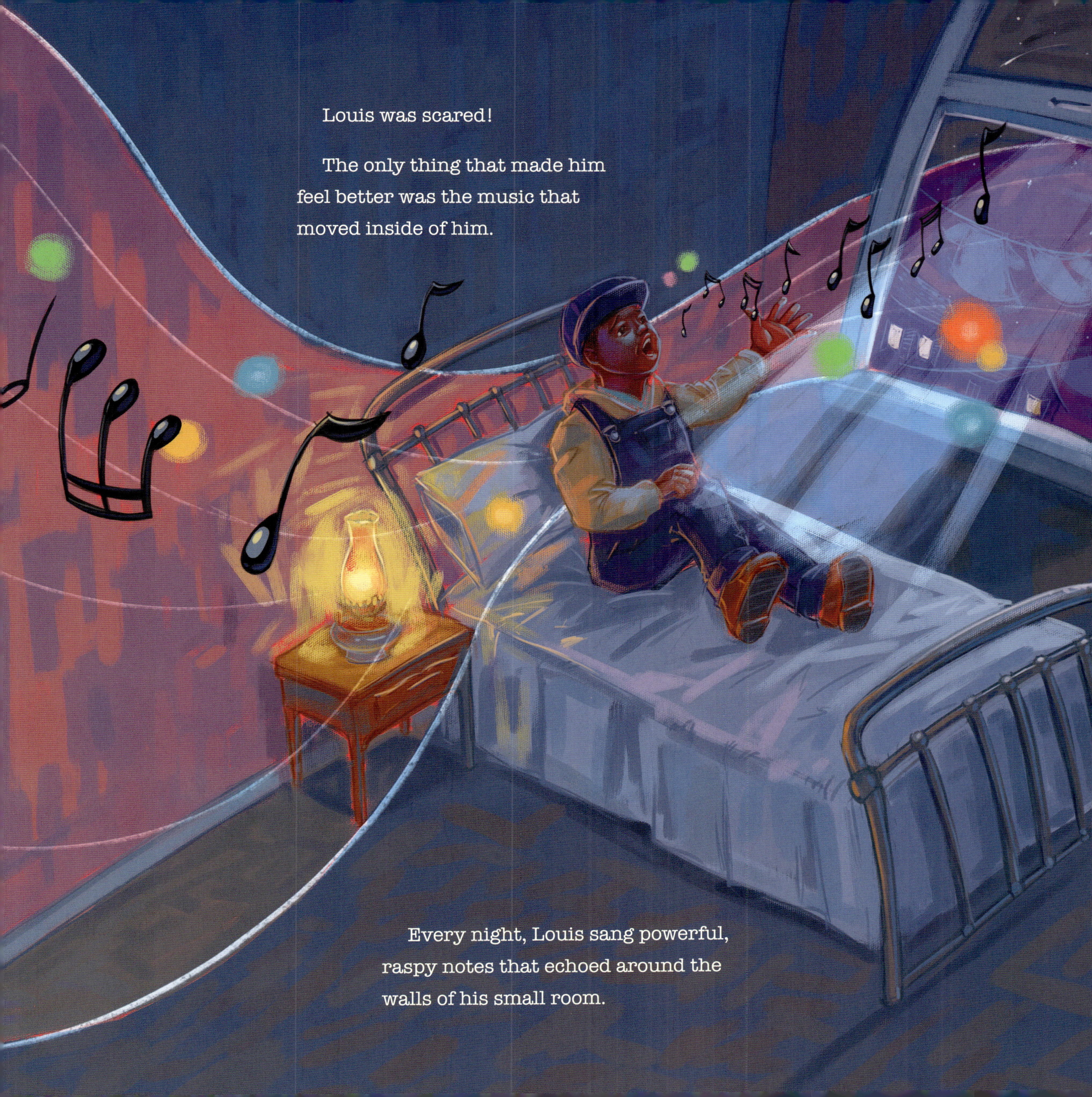

Louis was scared!

The only thing that made him feel better was the music that moved inside of him.

Every night, Louis sang powerful, raspy notes that echoed around the walls of his small room.

A teacher heard Louis and asked him if he could make a shiny brass instrument sing too.

So Louis decided to try something new. Louis played.

He made the trumpet sing just like he did! He played low notes that laughed:

PahPahPahPahPah!

He played fast notes that danced:

Dadadadadada!

He could bend the music notes and straighten them up again with his trumpet.

The other students cheered! Louis kept on playing.

After leaving school, Louis played all around the United States—from riverboats in New Orleans to jazz clubs in Chicago. The notes from his trumpet carried through the warm city nights.

Up east, Ella was singing her way to fame, performing all around New York City. She could throw music notes into the air and catch them back with her voice.

Ella had made a name for herself with her sweet voice. Louis did the same with his brassy trumpet. As their fame grew, their music reached all over the country. These two famous jazz musicians knew each other, but they had never had the chance to perform together. Until one night . . .

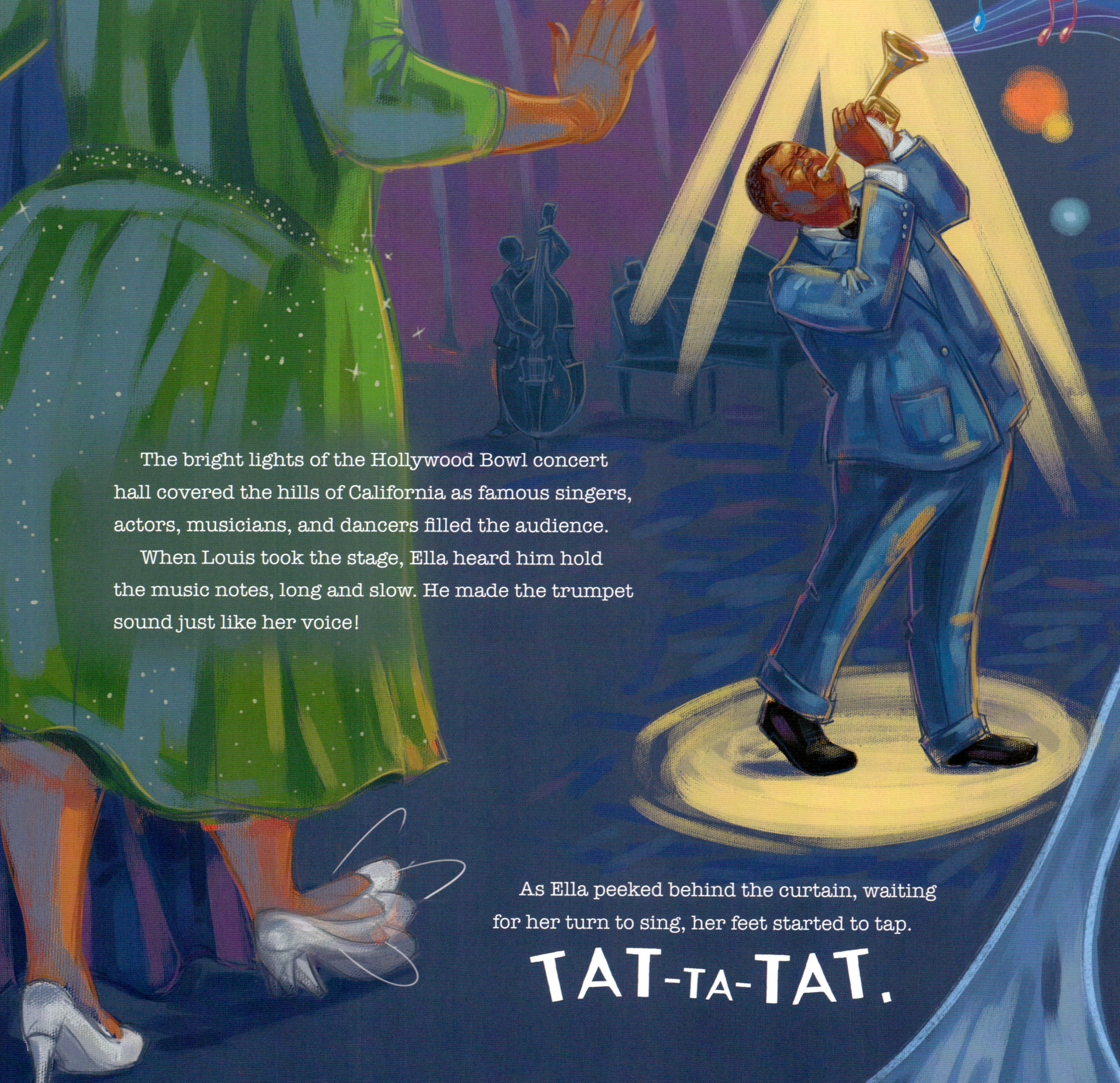

The bright lights of the Hollywood Bowl concert hall covered the hills of California as famous singers, actors, musicians, and dancers filled the audience.

When Louis took the stage, Ella heard him hold the music notes, long and slow. He made the trumpet sound just like her voice!

As Ella peeked behind the curtain, waiting for her turn to sing, her feet started to tap.

TAT-TA-TAT.

When Ella took the stage, Louis heard her move the notes up and down the scale like a rainbow. And when she started to scat—

"Do-bop-do-bop-do-bop-doo"

—she made her voice sound just like his instrument!

As Louis looked up from the audience, his fingers started to snap.

SNAP-PA-SNAP.

And then they took the stage together.
Louis held up his trumpet to his mouth.

Ella looked right at him and smiled.

Ella's voice sang staccato.

"Ba- da- da- da."

Louis's trumpet played legato.

Baaaaaaaaa-daaaaaaaaaa-daaaaaaaaa-daaaaaaad.

Ella danced in place as her voice scatted across the room.

"De- ba- do- ba- dee- ba- da-doo- da

Louis hugged his trumpet
and sang in a deep rumble.

"Baaa-bum-baaa-bum."

When Ella tossed a note with her voice,
Louis grabbed it back with his trumpet.
The music would push and pull,
push and pull.
Until the music notes started to swing.

The audience cheered and cheered.
Ella and Louis took a bow, together.

Soon they were performing on stages big and small—hopping on trains from New Orleans to New York, California to Chicago.

Ella's voice told stories as Louis's music painted pictures. Ella loved singing solo, and Louis loved playing alone with his trumpet, but making music together felt just right.

Today, if you ride a train up to Harlem, New York, you'll feel the tracks snapping and swaying, just like Ella's voice.

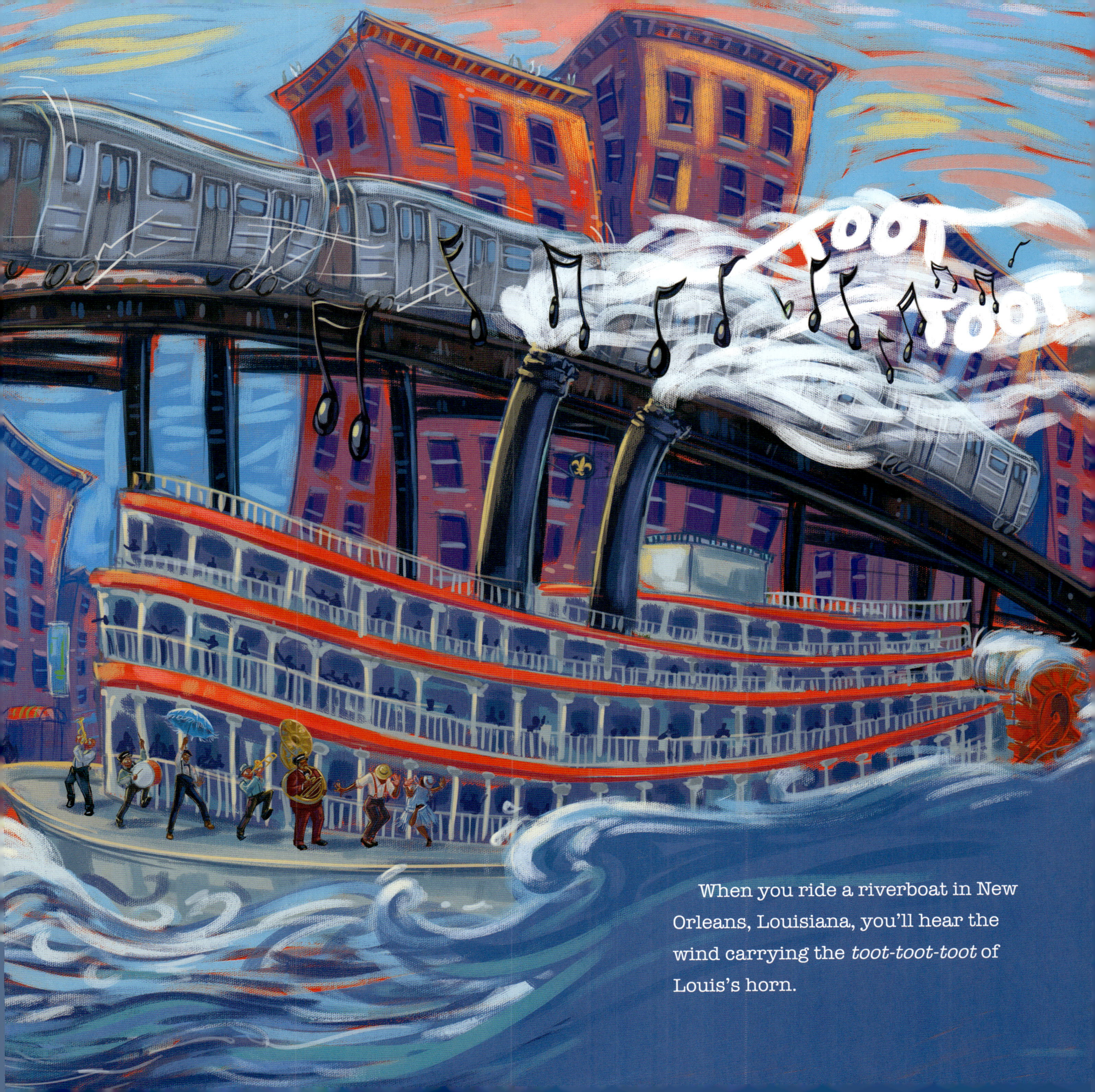

When you ride a riverboat in New Orleans, Louisiana, you'll hear the wind carrying the *toot-toot-toot* of Louis's horn.

But no matter where you are, when you feel the melody jump—then glide down; when you hear the notes leap off the scale only to find their way back home again: that's the sound of Ella and Louis's music playing on.

Author's Note

I have always loved music.

My mom says that when I was two years old, I would dance to the rhythm of the washing machine as it was swish-swish-swishing water around our clothes. She said I would shake my hips back and forth, to any steady beat—that I heard music all around me.

Music really is all around us, in different sounds, rhythms, pitches, beats. And when I first listened to recordings of Louis Armstrong playing the trumpet and Ella Fitzgerald singing, I realized that music isn't just around us—it is *in* all of us.

My favorite performances are when Louis Armstrong plays "What a Wonderful World" on the trumpet (and sings, too) and Ella Fitzgerald sings "Blue Skies" (and dances, too). And my favorite duet is when they perform "Cheek to Cheek." Both musicians make us feel the notes, the rhythms, the music in them and in us.

Importantly, each of these musicians brought new sounds to jazz music—an ability to make their instrument sound like a voice, or their voice sound like an instrument. And in this new sound—swing music—Ella and Louis played with the notes, making them longer or shorter than what was written on the page, making the notes move back and forth, like a swing! And with that, Ella Fitzgerald and Louis Armstrong changed the landscape of American music.

Louis was born in New Orleans in 1901, and Ella was born in Virginia about sixteen years later in 1917. Her family moved to New York soon after. With their age difference and the distance between them, Ella and Louis had individual experiences as up-and-coming artists, but once they got together, the parallels between their lives and journeys became clear.

Ella and Louis became famous for their ability to interpret music and connect with audiences in all contexts. They both rose to fame in the early 1900s in America, before the civil rights movement, when people were still separated because of their skin color. When Black people were not allowed to sing on certain stages. During his travels, Louis was often stopped by police just because of the way he looked. Once, after the popular Mocambo club in Hollywood rejected Ella multiple times because of her skin color, Ella had to get help from Marilyn Monroe to perform. Eventually, though, when Ella and Louis made music, everyone came to listen.

Ella and Louis toured all over the country, showing audiences how music can move above, beyond, and between skin colors, countries, and cultures. While they have collectively sold millions of albums, they only recorded three albums together: *Ella and Louis*, *Ella and Louis Again*, and *Porgy & Bess* (featuring songs from the famous opera of the same name). They recorded the first album the day after their first performance together at the Hollywood Bowl.

When Ella made her voice sound like a horn, Louis

sang back with his trumpet. When Louis improvised on the trumpet, Ella made her voice dance. Swing music got audiences to stand up and dance. Ella and Louis sang together, danced together, and captivated audiences together, creating a new sound and a new friendship.

It's like Ella sang in a famous song from her early days: "It don't mean a thing (if it ain't got that swing)." And the rest is jazz history.

Illustrator's Note

I've been listening to jazz music for over twenty-five years, and its rhythms, energy, and emotions have always been a source of inspiration for my artwork. I was first introduced to jazz from jazz samples that I heard in early nineties hip-hop songs. It sparked my curiosity and started my journey to learn more about jazz and the musicians who created this unique music form. Among the many great jazz musicians, Louis Armstrong and Ella Fitzgerald stand out as two of my favorites. Their voices and music have a way of making the heart dance, and I've tried to capture some of that magic in my illustrations. I hope that through these pages, you can feel the joy, the improvisation, and the spirit of jazz that they brought to life.

Sources

Armstrong, Louis. *Satchmo: My Life in New Orleans*. Boston, MA: Da Capo Press, 1986.

Jenkins, Sacha, dir. *Louis Armstrong's Black & Blues*. Apple TV, 2022.

Loudon, Christopher. "Ella Fitzgerald and Frank Sinatra." *Jazz Times*, April 25, 2019.

Nicholson, Stuart. *Ella Fitzgerald: A Biography of the First Lady of Jazz*. Boston, MA: Da Capo Press, 1995.

Teachout, Terry. *Pops: A Life of Louis Armstrong*. Boston, MA: Houghton Mifflin Harcourt, 2010.

For more information about Ella and Louis, visit www.ellafitzgerald.com and www.louisarmstronghouse.org.

Recommended Reading for Kids

Kirkfield, Vivian. *Making Their Voices Heard*. New York: Little Bee Books, 2020.

McDonough, Yona Zeldis. *Who Was Louis Armstrong?* New York: Penguin Random House, 2004.

Pinkney, Andrea Davis. *She Persisted: Ella Fitzgerald*. New York: Penguin Random House, 2023.

Sánchez Vegara, Maria Isabel. *Little People, Big Dreams: Ella Fitzgerald*. London: The Quarto Group, 2018.

BIRD LAND
SAVOY